CROOKED ASS ANNIE

AND

THE MYSTERY OF

THE MISSING CHILDREN

CROOKED ASS ANNIE

AND

THE MYSTERY OF

THE MISSING CHILDREN

A Short Humorous Mystery

Francis Bennett

Printed in the United States of America

This is a work of fiction. Names, characters, places, and
incidents either are the product of the author's imagination or
are used fictitiously. Any resemblance to actual persons,
living or dead, events, or locales, is entirely coincidental.

Cover Design by Tatiana Villa

ISBN 978-1484167137

ISBN -978-0-9892353-1-0 (e-book)

DEDICATED TO:

The People of Bay Shore

Long Island, New York

CROOKED ASS ANNIE

&

THE MYSTERY OF
THE MISSING CHILDREN

Everyone in town called her "Crooked-Ass Annie" except my mother, who wouldn't have such talk in her house. Even my father who was normally dignified about minorities and the down-trodden referred to the old lady as "Crooked-Ass Annie". He claimed she had been known by that name as long as he could remember, and no one had ever questioned the propriety of it. Even our mayor, Tom Connelly, in his Fourth of July speech last year referred to a long forgotten but important town historical event as having occurred

1

before the time of "Crooked-Ass Annie". This old woman and her nickname had worked their way into the folklore of the town so thoroughly that they had become a benchmark on the town's unofficial historical calendar. You had events that occurred in the time "before Crooked-Ass" and in the time "after Crooked-Ass".

I don't know how old Annie was when I first saw her hobbling down Main Street, but to an eight year old boy she appeared to be about a hundred and ten. She had dirty white hair that sprayed out from under the man's gray fedora she always wore. She was so bent over you couldn't tell how tall she was. She looked to be to be about four feet tall and must have weighed three hundred pounds. Her right hip was deformed so that it stuck out to one side forcing her torso to lean over to the opposite side. She balanced herself by resting her right hand on her deformed hip and sticking her right elbow in the air above the protruding hip. She waddled along bent over in this position.

Her demeanor was cranky and gruff and she seemed to take pleasure in scaring kids that came close to her on the street. "Get home where ya belong," she'd snarl as she passed you on the street. "Get home or I'll take ya home with me." That threat struck fear into the hearts of all young children in the town and was often repeated by frustrated parents who felt they were losing control of their unruly children.

"I can't handle you anymore I'm afraid,"
they'd sigh. "I guess I'll just have to send you
along to Crooked-Ass Annie's, and let her
straighten you out." That would be enough to
shock a kid into two weeks of exemplary conduct.
Banishment to Crooked-Ass Annie's was a fate
worse than death. No one, of course, ever actually
went to Annie's, and what's more, no one seemed
to know where she lived. The thought, however,
of Annie having at you with a free hand was the
recurring nightmare that played through the heads
of the youngsters in our town.

The threat of Annie was fortified by the
reality. Unlike fears of vampires, werewolves or
enormous apes that would fade into memory after
one night of bad dreams following the Saturday
matinee, the frightening folklore surrounding
Annie was constantly reinforced by actually
running into Annie on the street and having her
growl and snarl at you as you cowered in the
doorway of the drugstore or hid behind one of the
new litter baskets placed on every corner by the
town council.

"What are you lookin at, you goddamn little
snivel-nose? I eat kids bigger en you for dinner.
Get the hell outta here," she'd greet you. She had
a deep gravelly voice and was missing a tooth on
either side of her main front tooth, so her voice
and diction were punctuated with a spitting sound
that made her seem all the more onerous. She
carried a tattered cloth bag that was always full of
something, and she'd take a healthy swing at you

with it as she snarled, "skinny little boys like you ain't good for nuthin cept cryin like babies. Get the hell outta here fore I whack ya a good one," she'd growl as she took a swing with the bag. We'd squeeze out of the doorway and run a few quick paces down the block then stop and taunt the old lady.

"Crooked-Ass...Crooked-Ass...Crooked-Ass," we'd sing. "La..la...la...Crooked-Ass. Catch us if you can," we'd intone in our most annoying sing-song. She wouldn't even look back but just continue on her mysterious rounds to one store or another, filling the cloth bag with her necessaries, then head back to her secret lair. We often tried to follow, but she was a cagey old lady and would always find a way to shake us. One time we followed her all around town for over two hours when she led us to the hospital and went into the patients' area and never came out, so far as we could figure. Another time she completed her rounds at the Catholic Church and entered the dark interior never to emerge. A few days after that she led us to the junkyard up at the end of Bowers Road, and we figured we finally found her home. A three-hour search of every inch of that scary junkyard never uncovered a trace of Annie.

I asked my father where she lived. With a faraway look in his eye, he said, "That's one of the great unsolved mysteries of this town, my boy. Generation after generation has tried to find the home of Crooked-Ass Annie. None of them has, as far as I know."

4

"Come on, Pop. You're pullin my leg. Ya gotta be. She's a crippled old lady who's lived in this town since the dawn of history. Someone must know where she lives."

"Someone must, but no one seems to."

"Come on, Pop. You're teasing me, right?"

"I'm not teasing you, Crab, I don't know where Crooked-Ass Annie lives, and I don't know anyone who does, and that's gospel."

"Jeez Pop, that's weird. I can't believe it. Someone must be able to follow her home. She's a crippled old lady, for God's sake. It's ridiculous. I'm gonna find out where she lives," I concluded with great conviction.

"Why don't you just ask her? She's apt to tell you."

"Huh…well…yeah…never thought of that. I think I might just do that," I said bravely as I swaggered out of the room. I caught the look on my father's face over my shoulder out of the corner of my eye as I turned into the hall. His lips were slightly parted in a quiet smile as he nodded slowly up and down.

This one I had to do on my own. A crowd of kids following Annie around the streets would alert her too easily, and we would never find out where she spent the night. No, this had to be my first solo job, a sort of top secret effort. At first I thought doing it alone would take all the fun out it, but I found that the solitude and quiet planning heightened the sense of challenge and mystery and made the hunt for Annie's home more fun. It also made me feel more like a man. This wasn't kids' stuff. This wasn't foolin around. I could be the first kid in the history of Bay Shore to discover the secret of Crooked-Ass Annie; who she was; where she lived; how she had lived so long; did she have a weird and reclusive family tucked away in the woods somewhere? This was a real mystery, and I intended to solve it on my own.

School was out for the summer, so I had plenty of time to tail the old lady and learn her habits. I began the first day down in front of Oscar's candy store at the corner of Clinton and Main. Crooked-Ass Annie, common wisdom had it, walked past Oscar's every day at 7:55 in the morning on her way to mass at St. Patrick's Church directly across the street. She arrived right on time, and I followed her into the church and sat in the last pew, never letting the crazy old lady out of my sight. She sat in the first pew and prayed at the top of her lungs to the obvious annoyance of old Monsignor Walsh, the pastor.

"Our Father, who art in heaven," he began, and Annie followed half a word behind in a voice twice as loud as his. The resulting prayer sounded like an echo that was louder than the original sound.

"Our…OUR…fath…FATH…er…ER…who …WHO…art…ART…in…IN…hea…HEA…ven

....VEN..." until the pastor stopped and stared at a completely oblivious Annie caught up in a spell of piety. She, of course, continued without him, never noticing that he had stopped in frustration.

'HALLOWED BE THY NAME, THY KINGDOM COME, THY WILL BE DONE," she boomed at the silent pastor. Finally he realized that he was being left behind, and that he had lost control of the service. He was left with no alternative but to pick up the prayer wherever Annie was and to follow her lead to the end. His face became contorted with repressed anger as he mumbled the words of The Lord's Prayer under Annie's powerful spitting baritone. Annie finished with a dramatic, "AMEN", and a nod to the pastor signaling him to continue with the rest of the service. This condescending nod drove the pompous pastor into mortal combat with himself that was plainly visible to all the assembled faithful. His face turned bright red, and his head seemed to actually swell up as he fought for self-control. His eyes bulged out of their sockets as he sputtered slightly while fighting back the obvious urge to hurl himself on the old lady and throttle her. After a few unbearably tense moments the pastor let out a sort of whimper and walked back behind the altar to finish the service. Annie, of course, was oblivious to all of this.

About a half a minute before the pastor finished the final prayer Annie lost interest in the proceedings and began bumping and banging her way out of the pew until she had reached the center aisle. Once there, she turned toward the front doors with her enormous deformed rump facing back at the pastor and hobbled her way out of the church; a final and dramatic act of disrespect toward the pompous and now completely undone clergyman. He simply stood there staring at her rump as she waddled down the aisle and out the door. Then meekly he left the sanctuary himself.

As soon as the pastor left the altar I scrambled out the door in hot pursuit of the old lady. I was determined not to lose her trail.

"What the hell do ya think yer doin?" she snapped as I emerged from the dark church into the sunlight and almost bumped into her on the steps. I jumped back a foot and pressed my back against the church's door jam. "Ya following me ya little scamp? What d'ya expect to find, ya nosey little urchin? You'll find the back of me hand or the end of a sharp stick is what you'll find. Now get outta here before I take a dislike, ya skinny little bird-brained baby."

As she cocked back her cloth bag I jumped out of her reach and ran down the street about a half block before I felt completely safe. At the corner of Main and Maple I dodged into Whelan's drugstore for a soda. Stu Plummer, a senior at my high school, had the job of fountain boy.

"Hey, little guy. What can I get ya?" he greeted me.

"Don't call me little guy," I warned him immediately.

8

"Hey...okay...no   offense...big   guy
then...okay...how's that?"

"Come on, cut it out, Stu, will ya? I'm doin
something important here. I'm trailin Crooked-
Ass Annie. I'm finding out where she lives once
and for all; gimme a cherry coke."

"You're trailin Crooked-Ass Annie, a little
guy like you? Forget about it. Full grown men
can't find out where she lives, or who she is, or
what she's been doing around here all these years.
You think you're gonna find out just by walkin
around behind her; a little guy like you? Forget
about it, will ya?"

"What's the big deal, Stu? She's a crippled
old lady who hobbles around town. Why can't
anyone follow her?"

"We tried a couple of years ago. She's pretty
slippery. We followed her with a couple of guys,
and she'd always end up going someplace we
couldn't go, and then she'd always give us the
slip; like into a ladies room or a doctor's office or
the vault in a bank; places like that. We finally
got sick of the game and just gave up like
everybody else. You'll never figure her out, Crab.
Give up now."

"I'm given it a try, Stu. I'm real curious, and
I'm startin to get a little stubborn about it. Y'
know what I mean?"

"Yeah, I know what ya mean, but be careful,
okay? That old lady's dangerous. Ya never know
what she might have in store for a little kid like
you... Well...I don't mean little kid...I mean..."

"Forget it. I know what you mean. She's pretty scary lookin. What do ya figure she'd do to a kid if she got a hold of him in private?"

"I don't know really. But she's crazy as a hoot and mean as a rabid dog. She'd do something horrible; that's for sure."

"Yeah...I'm gonna find out where she goes though."

"Don't let yer curiosity get the better of ya, Crab. Over the years we got some missin kids in this town that ain't never been explained. All towns have missin kids, but we're the only town that has Annie, so I wouldn't be surprised if Annie had something to do with all those missin kids. Ya know, like they was curious and never came back from bein curious."

"What do ya mean 'missin kids'? What kids?"

"Kids missin over the years...no explanation...just missin. Down through the years there's been a lot of them. Kids here one day, missin the next. You know, *missin* kids."

"How many over how many years, Stu?"

"I don't know, but more than normal, I can tell ya that."

"Jeez...I never knew that. Missin kids huh?"

"Yup, kids missin all over the place. Crooked-Ass Annie if ya ask me."

Missin kids, I kept thinking as I walked home; kids missin; Annie...crazy old lady...hummm.

The **Bay Shore Sentinel** wasn't exactly **The New York Times,** but Edna Compton ran it like it was. She had regular editorial staff meetings with her lone reporter and printer, Jerry Butler. She wrote an opinionated editorial column every week that scolded some local dignitary or other for a minor infraction of her complex ethical or cultural standards. And she maintained a complete and up-to-date news "library" that consisted exclusively of past issues of the *Sentinel* filed in chronological order back to the beginning of time.

It was the library that interested me. Edna Compton cleaned off the old wide oak table in the middle of the *Sentinel's* offices that served as the library table, pointed to the thirty-six oak filing cabinets that lined the wall behind the table, and told me to help myself. I went back two years to 1954 and began my research from there. I figured that if any kids had been missing in Bay Shore more recently I would have heard about it and wouldn't need to be looking through old issues of **The Bay Shore Sentinel.**

1954 was clean. I looked at all 52 issues and found no mention of missing kids. It took an hour to go through a year. Since hard news was confined to the front page of **The Sentinel,** it was just a matter of pulling the issues out of the file and glancing at the front page. Returning each issue to its proper place was the big work, since

Edna Compton watched everything I did out of one eye while she ran the paper with the other.

1953 was another matter:

THE BAY SHORE SENTINEL
March 14, 1953

Winston Girl's Parents Report Her Missing To Police

The story went on to tell how Jennifer Winston, age 11, had not returned home from school, and after much frantic calling of friends and neighbors was reported missing to the police.

THE BAY SHORE SENTINEL
August 7, 1952

Rash of Runaways Continues

After a troubled summer of run-ins with the police and clashes with his parents, Johnny Turner's parents suspect that he has run away. No reports of foul play or *corpus delecti* indicate that

12

Johnny met with trouble. No, the article went on to reason, this appears to be another runaway much like the other two reported by parents in recent weeks. The new rebellious teenager syndrome seems to be sweeping Bay Shore and, indeed, the whole country. Maggie March and Bill Anter also seem to have rebelled and run away this summer. Their parents are very troubled so any information regarding Maggie's or Bill's whereabouts would be greatly appreciated...

1952 seemed to be a red letter year for kids turning up missing I thought. Neither article contained any information as to where these kids had last been seen or if anyone suspected foul play. Everyone in 1952 seemed to be taken with rebellious teenagers. I looked through the rest of the 1952 issues to see if any of these kids ever came back or were found but no mention of any of them ever appeared again. No more missing kids in 1952.

THE BAY SHORE SENTINEL
July 23, 1951

June Classen Feared Drowned

The Classen girl, age 12, was last seen swimming down at Kelly's Lake. She was never seen again and is feared drowned. The police have dragged the lake for three days, but no trace of her body has been found. This strikes the police as odd since other drownings at the lake over the years have always turned up a body. However, it is possible that her body got swept out to the deepest part of the lake by one of the mysterious

14

> underground currents
> reported in Kelly's
> Lake by marine
> scientists.

The subsequent ten weeks of issues turned up nothing more about the poor Classen girl. Another mysterious disappearance:

THE BAY SHORE SENTINEL
October 31, 1950

"Trick-Or-Treaters" Disappear

Two little girls out trick-or-treating never return. Looks like a kidnapping to local authorities but as yet no ransom demands have been made.

No ransom demands were ever made according to subsequent issues of *The Sentinel*.

No missing kids reported in 1950. After about three hours of hard detective work Edna Compton threw me out and closed the paper for the day. I dreamed about missing kids that night.

I worked down at *The Sentinel* for two more days going all the way back to 1940. In fourteen

15

years over twenty kids had disappeared from Bay Shore without a trace. Each story was different and had its own plausibility, so between runaways and kidnappings no one seemed to notice how many we had lost. I pointed this out, first to Edna Compton as long as I was right there with her, but she just asked me what I made of it. Since I didn't know what to make of it I didn't bother speculating about foul play or Annie. I figured I'd keep that to myself until I had more evidence. I was completely convinced that, not only was the disappearance of twenty kids over fourteen years pretty abnormal, but also that Annie had something to do with it.

I began trailing Annie again the next morning. I didn't bother attending the painful church service but simply waited outside until the service was over, and Annie came out to go about her chores for the day. She came out grumbling and mumbling to herself as she waddled down Main Street toward Bunger's grocery market. I followed about fifty paces behind taking no chance that she'd spot me again. She entered Bunger's and immediately accosted Mr. Bunger, who hadn't seen her coming.

"Bunger...where the hell'd ya get these measly little marble-sized potatoes? They're no goddamn good. Ya expect me to buy these? That'll be the day! What the hell ya expect me to feed myself? What kind of grocer are ya...ya here to starve people to death? I can get better food out of the garbage cans behind Maple Avenue...marble

16

potatoes, for Christ's sake, Bunger. What the hell are ya up to?"

"Good morning, Miss Ann. How are you today?" Bunger greeted the old woman with a calm smile. You'd never know he had heard a word she said. "How about a couple ears of this beautiful corn I got in this morning from Slatery's farm, just the thing for ya?"

"If I wanted corn I woulda asked for it. Potatoes, you old buzzard, I want potatoes." Annie walked away from Bunger and went about her shopping just as Bunger, in his wisdom, knew she would. She took two ears of corn, one tomato, one head of iceberg lettuce and one turnip and put them all in her cloth bag as she went. It was Bunger's job to watch what she selected and charge her the appropriate amount when she left the store. She never bothered to go through the checkout stand. When she had finished selecting her vegetables she headed for the door where Bunger intercepted her and asked for three dollars and twenty cents. She paid without comment and headed down the street toward Klein, the butcher.

Three of the local housewives were already in Klein's shop when Annie struggled through the door and waddled up to the counter. With her right hand planted firmly on her deformed hip and her torso bent down to the level of the windows in the meat display counter, Annie studied each and every piece of meat that Klein had on display. The gentle women of the town had interrupted their conversation upon Annie's entrance and now stood to one side waiting for their orders as Annie inspected the meat counter slowly from one end to the other. They watched her with fear and trepidation knowing that one false move could set loose her tongue, and that they would get a lashing from Annie it would take them a week to get over.

"Pig's knuckles," Annie finally said to no one in particular. "I don't see any pig's knuckles; no knuckles, Klein?"

"No knuckles, Annie, not today," Klein called from behind the counter, invisible as he bent to his butchery for the three housewives waiting in the corner.

"Huumm..." replied Annie. "Gimme a good slab of tongue meat, Klein...no knuckles...tongue then," she concluded with a grunt and a nod of her head. Her order placed, she returned to her bent-over position, and in doing so, noticed the shoes and the dress hems of the three petrified women hiding in the corner. She tilted her head back so that she could see them from under the fedora brim, took one quick look, shrugged and turned back toward Klein behind the counter. "Tongue for these three, too, Klein. Peers they need it," she grunted as she shuffled out to the front of the shop and sat on the wooden bench outside the door.

After about five minutes Klein brought out Annie's tongue all wrapped in butcher paper, and she paid him without further comment. She hefted herself off the bench and started back up Main Street toward the church and the way she had come from home. I was in hiding across the street behind some maple trees, and when she started for home I could feel the anxiety begin to build in my stomach. She hadn't seen me yet, I knew, and if she didn't there would be no need for her to take any evasive action. She would probably just go home with her groceries. As she waddled back up Main Street I followed at a safe distance. She walked slowly with one hand on her protruding hip and the other holding the cloth bag barely off the ground. She wore a gray wool cardigan sweater over her old red and blue cotton house dress. The fedora and her white hair completed the ensemble giving her a certain pitiable appearance, and I found myself feeling sorry for her as I followed her out to the edge of town and down the country road toward the lake. With the wind gently blowing the faded dress, and Annie hobbling along at a snail's pace, she looked just like any other old, lonely woman. Suddenly I couldn't remember why I suspected her of high crimes and misdemeanors. I had an impulse to run and catch up with her and offer to carry the cloth sack. In fact, I was about to do just that when I looked ahead and saw her make a turn into the woods that bordered the road on the south side. By the time I arrived at the place she had turned in, she was gone. I rushed into the woods and searched for a trail or a path or any sign of her passage. There was none. She had vanished. I searched that whole section of woods until nightfall with no success. Annie was gone without a trace.

Darkness enshrouded the woods faster than I had expected. Everything I looked at began to appear sinister and slightly out of focus as the night shadows made new shapes between bushes, shrubs and trees. I don't know how far into the woods I wandered, but I suddenly realized that I wasn't sure where I was and had no idea how to retrace my steps and get back to the road before it was completely black. I think the slight night breeze snapped me out of my intense search for Annie, because I remember feeling a chill at first and then realizing I was lost. I spun around immediately and tried to remember my route into the woods, but nothing in my sight seemed familiar. My vision was no longer distinct and clear. The descending night had washed all color from the scene. Shadows and dark clumps had replaced bushes and paths. The night breeze created new movement among the branches and brought the woods around me to life. I turned three hundred and sixty degrees, slowly peering into the woods around me, trying to discern something familiar and comforting. I felt my breathing start to quicken and get erratic, and I knew I was starting to panic. I took one huge deep breath in an effort to steady my nerves and, rather than stare into the dark woods around me, I looked up into the night sky and watched the wispy clouds scoot past the now bright three-quarter moon.

Calm down and think, I told myself. You couldn't be more than a hundred yards into the woods. When a car goes by on the road you'll hear it, and you can walk in that direction. Now just calm down and sit under a tree and use your sense of hearing to guide you.

With my hand out in front of me I took a few steps over to the oak tree I knew was there, but could now only see the outline of, and sat down against the trunk to rest my senses and my legs. The trunk and the ground around it were still warm from the heat of the day's sun, and the warmth gave me comfort and made me feel safe. I sat there quite still, looking first at the darkened woods around me, then at the night sky and the bright moon. I felt like whistling, but I didn't. I just sat there listening. Darkness makes your hearing more acute. I could hear the branches rustling, the squirrels moving in the trees and occasionally a larger animal, like a possum or a muskrat, moving along the ground. I was waiting for a car to go by to set my internal compass toward the road, but one never did. I wasn't wearing a watch, but it seemed like an hour passed while I sat and listened. I remember feeling tired from the day's tracking of Annie, and I started yawning and stretching and in a few minutes I fell asleep.

Then I heard it. First it seemed like a beautiful female voice humming in the distance and carried faintly to my ear. No, it was a high-pitched bell tingling gently in the night breeze or perhaps a whole chorus of well-trained children singing a hymn many miles away. Yes...Yes...that's it...a chorus of children. Gradually I began to discern the distinct voices; the girls'... high-pitched but clear and resonant, and the little boys'... just as high-pitched as the girls' but so tight that they tingled and shimmered behind the clarity of the girls' perfect pitch.

"Together...Together...Forever Together..." they sang just above the wind.

"Together...Together...Forever Together..." a second group of voices replied in the same melody.

I couldn't believe my ears and slowly peeked around the trunk of the tree I was sitting against to try to get a glimpse of who was singing. As my head cleared the tree trunk I could see a faint white light spreading out below the chest-high mist that had formed in the night woods. The mist swirled around the bushes and trees giving the forest an eerie, ghostly feel, while under the moving mist white footlights steadied the ground and created a feeling of expectation, as if something important was about to happen. I could not see where the light came from. It was just there, illuminating the ground below the mist, covering an area about twenty yards wide. The singing continued to become clearer but not louder, which made me feel that the singers were moving toward me.

'FOREVER......FOREVER......FOREVER.......
.FOREVER," they sang in the most beautifully harmonized choral tones you can imagine. Listening to the music as it came closer and closer, I pulled my head back in behind the tree trunk. The fear I had felt earlier began to subside as I rested my head against the warm tree trunk and waited with resignation for the chorus to surround me.

The ground light began to leak around the base of the tree. It oozed around the trunk but continued straight past me on either side, leaving me trapped but safely hidden in the darkness of the long narrow shadow cast by the tree. I could sense that the singing filled the light area around me with great volume, but the intensity did not penetrate the darkness of my shadow. I could clearly hear the singing, but the volume in the shadow was soft and low, while the light area pulsated with the children's high-pitched voices. I could see nothing more than the beautiful white ground light under the forbidding and cold swirling mist of the night fog that had enshrouded the entire woods. The now booming voices continued to leak softly into my shadow.

"......WE...WANDER..TOGETHER......
TOGETHER...WE...WANDER.......TOGETHER
FOREVER, FOREVER, FOREVER." I could sense the ear-shattering volume of the sound in the light but could hear only the most tender and modulated tones. I dared not move because I sensed that if I stepped out of the shadow into the

light, the crushing volume of the sound would pierce my eardrums and shatter my sanity. I sensed that the light would not erase my shadow and crush me to death with the sound as long as I did not violate the border between light and shadow, so I sat as they sang. I watched as the promising ground light did not eradicate the swirling darkness and listened to soft and beautiful children's voices soothe me in the shadow but destroy all existence in the light. I stared straight ahead at the long narrowing shadow. Although the shadow disappeared from my vision at a point in the distance, I knew that the light did not merge and obliterate the shadow. It continued into infinity.

As I stared into my endless shadow I saw her. She walked slowly toward me, only movement at first, then a small vague moving image...then Annie. I did not recognize her immediately. She stood erect, ramrod straight. The man's fedora was gone and her white hair was combed out and flowing over her shoulders and down her back. She smiled for the first time and had all her teeth, and when she spoke her voice was no longer raspy but musical and deep.

"You have chosen to join the missing children. You will leave your family and the world you know and join me and the children in the light. You need only cross the boundary between shadow and light, and we will be together forever." Her eyes were bright, and she smiled at me as she offered her invitation, but somehow I knew that to cross into the light was to be crushed by the inhuman decibel of the children's chorus.

"Who are you?" I asked trying to buy time. "Where am I? Where is Annie?" She smiled at me again and I knew that this was Annie... and she knew that I knew it.

"You are in the middle, Mr. Crabber, and you must choose. Your curiosity has led you this far. Now you must choose to step into the light or to remain in the shadow. The answers you seek are in the light; satisfaction eludes those who remain in shadow. Join me in the light." She had come pretty close to me now and was reaching out her hand for me to take it and follow her over the boundary between light and shadow. She startled me. I jumped back and hit my head against the trunk of the tree I had been leaning on.

"Aoww...oh...jeez," I sputtered after hitting my head. "Look lady, I don't know what you're talking about, and I'm not sure what's going on around here, but I'm going to be running along now, if you don't mind."

I was trapped, of course, by the tree behind me, the light on both sides and Annie blocking my escape down the center of the shadow. I was getting pretty scared, but I was trying not to show it. Annie was staring directly at me now, and her eyes were beginning to glow. Her entire body slowly floated into the air a few inches off the ground. Suddenly she waved her arms like an orchestra leader, and the volume of sound from outside the shadow doubled and scared me to death.

"YOU WILL JOIN THE MISSING CHILDREN," she boomed over the music. "This is your reward for seeking the truth." The chorus continued at the increased volume as she floated there in front of me, and I could feel myself starting to cry.

"The missing children are dead," I shouted. "I know they're dead. I do not want to join them. Let me go," I shrieked as she waved her arms and increased the music to almost deafening proportions. I covered my ears and fell to my knees as the pain became unbearable. My head was pounding, and the pain in my ears was making me nauseous as the chorus continued,

"TOGETHER...TOGETHER..TOGETHER.... .TOGETHER..."

No longer able to stand the pain, I sprang to my feet and ran directly at Annie down the center of the shadow. I ran right through her, or she stepped out of the way, I'm not sure which, but I kept running down the center of the shadow, blinded by pain, but avoiding the light on both sides as I stumbled over rocks and shrubs.

"Run...Run...Run," I screamed to myself silently as I drove myself down the shadow. Don't stop running. "Go...Go...Go." Suddenly I tripped over a log lying across the path and plunged head first into the road, hitting my head on the blacktop and knocking myself unconscious.

I awoke the next morning with a headache and a deep bloody scab across the top of my left eye. It was that time of the early morning just before the sun comes up when it's light out, but the sun isn't visible yet. I lay still for a few minutes looking at the red morning sky, when suddenly I realized where I was and what I had been through. I rolled over and pushed myself to my feet and looked at the woods around me. I tried to remember if my nightmare had been real. The bump on my head was real enough, and my pants were dirty and snagged and pulled reminding me of my escape from the woods.

I started back down the country road toward town realizing that I had never stayed out all night before without telling my parents where I'd be. They were going to be pretty upset. I quickened my step thinking about my mother's worry. I got home about seven, and my parents were upset alright. They seemed pretty glad to see me though, so I just told them I was hiking in the woods out on the old country road and had tripped and fallen, hitting my head on a rock. I said I was okay though, and sorry I had worried them. My mother whipped me up a pretty good 'welcome home' breakfast, which she figured could cure anything. After the pancakes and eggs I took a bath, changed into some fresh clothes, and headed down to McNulty's field to try and pick up a game of baseball.

It was a little early for any of the other guys from the neighborhood to play ball, so I just sat on the rickety old bleachers and tossed the ball up in the air while I waited. After about ten minutes I saw her hobbling across the field from the Clinton Avenue side. I knew it was Crooked-Ass Annie when she was still a hundred yards away. She was bent over carrying her cloth bag. She moved pretty slowly giving me plenty of time to run away. I couldn't move. I sat stone-still and watched her approach. She crossed at about the middle of the diamond right over the second base pad. She was heading for the opening in the fence behind first base that led out to Main Street. I was sitting on the bleachers behind third base. When she was about halfway between first and second base she called out to me.

"No one to play with, huh?"

I didn't answer.

She stopped walking.

I stopped breathing.

"Cat got yer tongue?" she called as she looked back over her shoulder in my direction.

I didn't answer.

"You goddamn little skinny kids are all alike, scared of yer own goddamn shadow. I'm not gonna bite ya. What the hell, yer too goddamn skinny, anyway. Go find some friends to play with ya. Go on, get the hell outta here."

I just sat still.

28

"Ya heard me. Go on. Get outta here."

I still didn't move.

Finally Annie just shook her head and continued on her journey toward first base and the gate out to Main Street. Just as she reached first base, she stopped again. She looked over her shoulder at me but didn't say anything. She bent down and slowly wrote something in the dirt next to the first base pad. Then she straightened up to her normal bent-over position and hobbled out the gate and up Main Street.

I decided a long time ago not to tell you what she wrote in the dirt. I figured you wouldn't believe me, or you'd think I was nuts or something. Now I'm a few years older, and people don't think I'm as immature as I was, so I need to tell somebody what she wrote. I figure it makes some kind of difference, but I'm not sure what.

After Annie left the ball field, I slid off the bleachers and walked slowly over to first base to see what she had left in the dirt. In clear, legible, two-inch block letter, she had written:

TOGETHER
FOREVER

ABOUT THE AUTHOR

Francis Bennett was educated in a Catholic seminary and at the Harvard Business School. This curious combination gave birth to his unusual view of life and his humorous take on all things profound to profane. He is currently working at his home in Scottsdale, Arizona on his second collection of "Quit School" lessons learned along life's humorous path.

www.francisbennettbooks.com

Excerpt From:

THE BOOKBAG UK INTERVIEWS THE AUTHOR

BB: You've said the location of the stories is fictional but it does seem very real. Is it loosely based on any particular place? Does it relate back to your childhood?

FB: The location of the stories is Bay Shore, Long Island, New York, the town where I grew up. The fictional disclaimer at the beginning of the book is there as a matter of form since I fictionalized a very real place. All the characters are based on actual people who populated my boyhood but I portrayed them with some literary license. I loved them all. I remain grateful to them for all they did for me simply because of who they were.

BB: I too grew up in the 1950's and it did seem that children had a lot more freedom then. Do you think this is true? Do you have good memories of your own childhood?

FB: As you can see in the book, I have wonderful memories of my childhood. My parents had just lived through the depression and World War II. They were determined to build a normal, respectable life for themselves and their family. From that psychic place they didn't fear small dangers or expect life to unfold without trauma so they weren't nearly as protective of us as we became of our children.

CROOKED ASS ANNIE is taken from **QUIT SCHOOL!** A collection of humorous short stories by Francis Bennett available at: Amazon , Barnes and Noble, iBooks and Smashwords.

Made in the USA
Charleston, SC
07 June 2013